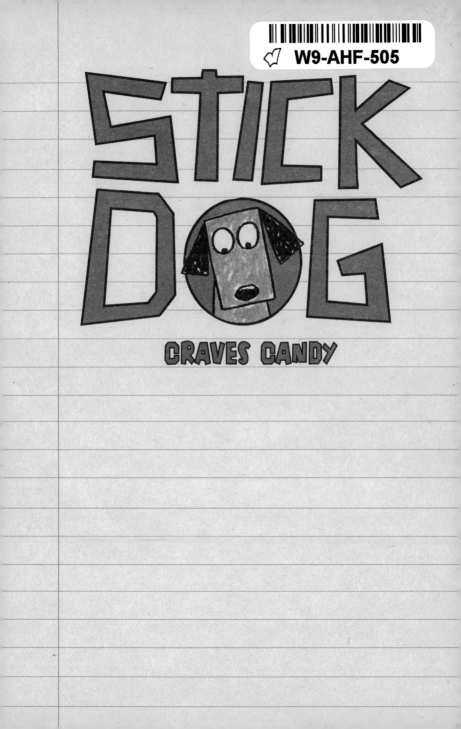

STICK DOG

CRAVES CANDY

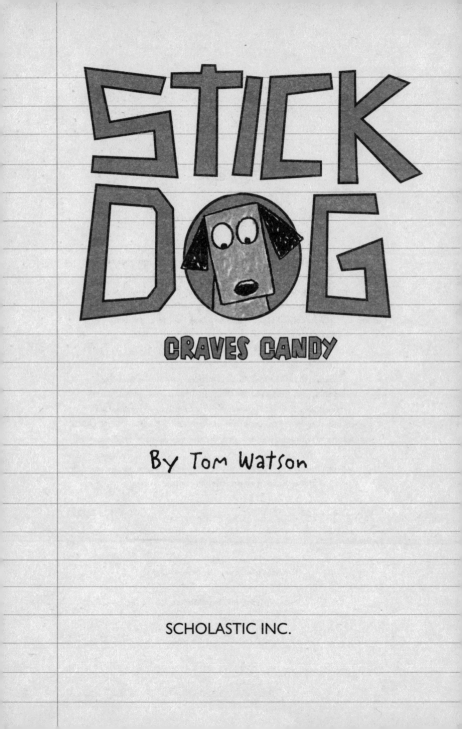

STICK DOG

CRAVES CANDY

By Tom Watson

SCHOLASTIC INC.

To Stephanie

ISBN 978-1-338-34997-9

12 11 10 9 8 7 6 5 4 3   18 19 20 21 22 23

Printed in the U.S.A.   40

First Scholastic printing, October 2018

Typography by Jeff Shake

TABLE OF CONTENTS

Chapter 1: Did Stick Dog Move His Pipe?   7

Chapter 2: The Smells of Autumn   21

Chapter 3: The Color of Cheetos   31

Chapter 4: What Stripes Saw   46

Chapter 5: Stew Ingredients   66

Chapter 6: Candy Is Dandy   83

Chapter 7: Attack of the Cherry Pits   103

Chapter 8: Flufforable   114

Chapter 9: Poodlesaurus Rex   130

Chapter 10: Stuck   145

Chapter 11: Bart, Ruth, Ralph,
              and Adam (and Karen)   154

Chapter 12: Stick Dog Plants Himself   166

Chapter 13: Take One, Please   187

CHAPTER 1

DID STICK DOG MOVE HIS PIPE?

It was early evening and Stick Dog was asleep in his pipe.

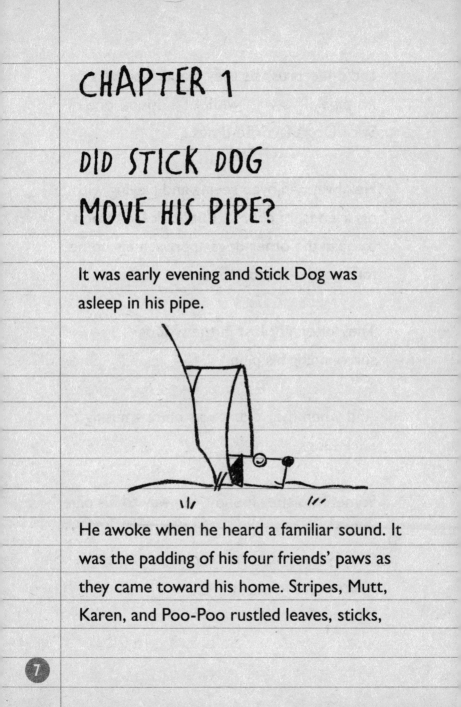

He awoke when he heard a familiar sound. It was the padding of his four friends' paws as they came toward his home. Stripes, Mutt, Karen, and Poo-Poo rustled leaves, sticks, and underbrush as they made their way to his pipe. This was, without a doubt, one of Stick Dog's favorite times.

He always enjoyed seeing and playing with his friends, of course. But Stick Dog loved to hear the other dogs approach his home for another reason too.

They often got lost in the woods surrounding his pipe.

And when they did, it was quite amusing to Stick Dog.

Sometimes they found their way to his pipe in five minutes, and sometimes it took them twenty minutes. The record was an entire afternoon.

The best part for Stick Dog was that he could hear little comments his friends made to each other as they sought his pipe. And this day was no exception. Stick Dog could hear them talking fifty yards to the left.

"I think Stick Dog moved his pipe again," said Karen, the dachshund.

"That's the third time this week," Mutt added.

Stick Dog smiled to himself and coughed a couple of times to give away his location a little bit.

COUGH!

"I hear him!" said Karen.

"Me too!" said Mutt. "It's this way."

In a couple of minutes—and several more coughs—Karen, Poo-Poo, Stripes, and Mutt emerged from the forest in front of Stick Dog's pipe.

"Stick Dog," Karen said, and squatted down to brush burrs from her fur with her front paws. "You have to stop moving your pipe! It makes it too hard for us to find."

Stick Dog glanced up at the roof of his pipe and then all the way around the rim of its opening. It was a huge pipe. It was probably eight feet high and it ran all the way under Highway 16, which was a four-lane highway about one hundred feet above them.

"I didn't move it," said Stick Dog. "I couldn't. It's at the bottom of this giant hill and it goes all the way through it. There must be two hundred tons of dirt and rocks above this thing. How could I possibly move it?"

"Well, it's not where it was yesterday," said Stripes, the Dalmatian, agreeing with Karen.

"Of course it is."

"I concur with Karen and Stripes," said Mutt. "If it was where it was yesterday, then we would have found it much quicker."

"Yes," said Stick Dog. "You would think so."

"A-HA!" yelped Poo-Poo, the poodle. "You admitted it! You've been moving your pipe!"

Stick Dog shook his head and wondered if it was worth continuing the conversation. He decided it was. "I didn't admit moving the pipe—I agreed that you should be able to find the pipe if I *hadn't* moved it."

"Umm, I know a thing or two about logic," said Karen. She scooched her belly across the ground, trying to scrape a final burr from her fur. "And you just proved yourself wrong, Stick Dog. First, you said we should be able to find your pipe. Second, we couldn't find it. Therefore, the pipe must have moved."

"Excellent deductive reasoning, Karen!" Mutt exclaimed. "Way to figure it out."

"Yes, yes," Stripes said.

And Poo-Poo pointed a paw directly at Stick Dog. He smiled slightly from one side of his mouth. He squinted one eye and declared in a loud, sharp whisper, "You're busted!"

Now, Stick Dog could have said, "Maybe you guys just aren't very good at finding things in the woods." Or he could have asked, "How in the world could I pull a huge pipe out from under a two-hundred-ton hill of rocks and dirt?" Or he could have said, "You guys are nuts."

But Stick Dog didn't say any of those things.

He liked the looks on their faces. They expressed a sense of accomplishment. Stick Dog was often the one who ended up being right about things—whether it was some piece of random information or the legitimacy of a particular food-snatching strategy. And now that the other dogs thought they had gotten the best of him (even though Stick Dog knew they hadn't), he liked the way they were feeling about themselves.

So Stick Dog let them believe that he had moved his pipe just to trick them. And he changed the subject entirely by saying this: "I'm hungry. We need to find some food."

Food is, by the way, the one-and-only best

way to get a dog's attention. And I'm not just making this up for the story's sake.

Do you want proof about this dog characteristic?

Okay.

Find a dog and have some cheese or little pieces of chicken with you.

 Now, give that dog a favorite toy—a tennis ball, a chewed-up rope, maybe an old baseball cap . . . whatever. Let him get used to having that toy. Let him gnaw on it and snuggle with it.

We'll use the baseball cap as an example.

Here's what they're thinking: "Man, this baseball cap is the absolute best! I can't believe they gave it to me! They used to wear this thing on their heads and now it's mine. Why would they want to cover up their only patch of fur anyway? I don't understand these humans. They're loony. Oh, never mind. I've got this cap and it's chewy and flexible and everything I love! It doesn't taste too good, but who cares?! I think I'll swallow little pieces of it later anyway. Woo-hoo!"

The dog loves this cap, right?

Now, do this: put a single piece of cheese or a little piece of chicken on the floor about ten feet away. Make sure the dog sees you, but you don't have to call him or point to the food or anything.

Now watch what happens.

Ninety percent of all dogs will drop the cap—that just nanoseconds ago was the absolute center of their universe—and go get that food.

You know what the other 10 percent do?

They're the smart ones. They take that baseball cap over to the food on the floor. Then they drop the cap right next to the food, eat the food, and pick the cap back up. But make no mistake: it's the food they

want the most. Need further proof for this
10 percent of Einstein dogs?

All right, Mister or Missus I-don't-believe-
everything-I-read-in-a-book. Try this: get
the dog to "stay," then take the baseball cap
and put it on the floor a few feet away to
the left of the dog. Then take the tasty food
morsel and put it on the floor a few feet
away to the right. And then say, "Okay"
to release this fine beast and see where he
goes first.

He will go to the
food. Every time.
Guaranteed.

If he doesn't go to the food first,
I'm afraid I have some bad news for you.
Here it is:

What you have there in front of you is *not* a dog. I don't know what it is (HOW COULD I? I'M NOT EVEN THERE?!?), but it is most certainly not a dog. It may be a big rabbit—or a hamster. Or maybe it's your little sister or brother dressed up in a dog costume to fool you. Younger siblings always do stuff like that.

THIS IS
NOT
A DOG.

Whatever it is, it is not a dog. So, you should go to your parents and say, "I want a dog." And when they say, "We already have a dog," you say, "No, we don't. This whatever-it-is does not prioritize food over its favorite toy. Therefore, it is not a dog. And I want a dog!"

Use the highly scientific toy-versus-food test to prove everything to your parents. They might not be convinced, but they will appreciate your scientific methods.

So, yeah, anyway.

When Stick Dog said he was hungry, that was it. There was no more talk of him moving the giant pipe. Now the dogs were focused completely on food—or, more precisely, their lack of food. Rising above the whisper of the wind through the birch and sycamore trees, above the rustle and crackle of leaves, beyond the steady and rhythmic beat of traffic high above on Highway 16, a more pronounced and significant sound could be heard.

The stomach rumblings of five hungry dogs.

CHAPTER 2

THE SMELLS OF AUTUMN

Stick Dog raised his nose in the air and sniffed toward Picasso Park, a common hangout for the dogs and the place where they had once eaten several tasty, juicy hamburgers. He didn't smell anything grilling, but he wanted confirmation and asked Poo-Poo, "Can you smell anything? Anybody grilling out?"

Poo-Poo had gained a reputation for having the best nose of the bunch—and rightfully so. For not only could Poo-Poo smell aromas from a great distance, he could also identify and describe the smells perfectly and in great detail. It was a job he took very seriously—and Stripes, Mutt, Karen, and Stick Dog awaited his report.

Poo-Poo closed his eyes, lifted his nose in the air, and did two very slow circles, sniffing and snorting the whole time. When he finally stopped revolving, he opened his eyes and spoke.

"I'm sorry to report," he began, "that there is nobody grilling at the park. I detect not a single whiff of smoky hamburger goodness. Likewise, there is nobody grilling any frankfurters, hot dogs, wieners, franks, metts, red hots, weenies, or coneys."

"Aren't those all just different names for frankfurters?" Karen asked.

Poo-Poo smirked a little at this suggestion. "Perhaps to the unsophisticated, yes."

Poo-Poo suddenly snapped his head in the exact opposite direction. The others could tell some stray smell had drifted past his nose. "I am getting one familiar scent though. It's about fifty-three paces forward and slightly to the left. Near the trunk of that old birch tree by the creek."

Stick Dog knew that old birch tree quite well. He had often sat by it on hot summer days to take advantage of its shade and the cool breeze that blew across the surface of the creek water. He was certain there was no food around there. "You smell something to eat over there?"

"It's something. Something familiar," whispered Poo-Poo. He closed his eyes, concentrating even harder. "I just can't put my paw on it."

Now he had aroused the interest of the other dogs even more, and they edged closer to him.

"What is it? What is it?" asked Stripes.

Then Poo-Poo opened his eyes and turned quickly toward Mutt. "Were you over by that old birch tree a little while ago?"

Mutt began to shake his head, then stopped and began to nod slowly. "Yes. Yes, I was."

"Did you have to go to the bathroom?"

"Of course," said Mutt. "I'm a dog. I have to go to the bathroom all the time. I can't help it—with all these tree trunks around and everything. What am I supposed to do? Not go? That's impossible."

Now, to you and me, this might not make a whole lot of sense. But to a bunch of dogs, it was a perfectly logical explanation.

"Forget it," sighed Poo-Poo. "I was just catching Mutt's scent."

With Poo-Poo's sniffing complete, Stick Dog was ready to go. It was time to find some food.

"Okay," he declared. "Let's get moving. We need to find something to eat."

Without hesitation, Stick Dog and his four
friends ran through the woods toward
where all the humans lived.

Autumn is not a good time for the five dogs
to find food. It's too cool for people to grill.
And with kids in school, frankfurter carts,
ice cream trucks, and things of that sort
were nowhere to be seen.

And there was another problem. While it
was too cool to grill, the autumn breeze did
provide human families a chance to open
their windows a bit to allow fresh air into
their homes.

When some of that fresh air was let in—
some of that inside air was let out. And
when that inside air was let out during
dinnertime, many of the mouth-watering
aromas drifted and danced through the air,
teasing the dogs' noses—and stomachs.

And the worst part of all?

Autumn dinners are the absolute best.

Think about it. Summer is the time for
sandwiches and grilling and grabbing
something fast so you can go back outside
and play. Spring is all about the Earth waking
up and new sprouts emerging, and we all
eat like rabbits—lettuce and berries. And in
winter, there's nothing growing—and your
teeth are too busy chattering to eat anyway.

But autumn. Oh, autumn.

That's when the meals get hearty and warm. The drop in temperature makes us want to have thick soups and stews to heat us up. We want warm biscuits and thick bread to soak up all the extra liquid in our bowls. We want to eat big meals because we think there's a chance we will hibernate through winter. Potatoes, corn on the cob, turkey, and pumpkin pie.

= AUTUMN

I *love* pumpkin pie.

So, when the dogs emerged from the woods, a lot of those hearty scents drifted from windows all around them. And it made their hunger even worse.

It was dusk, a very good time to embark on a food search. The evening was growing dark and people were mostly home from school and work.

As he moved slowly and carefully from the forest, Stick Dog looked left and right and all around. "No humans," he said to the other four behind him. "We'll follow the strongest food scent. Then, we'll make a plan. Poo-Poo, could you find the tastiest scent around here?"

"Indeed I can," Poo-Poo answered immediately and with supreme confidence.

"Just give me a minute."

The scent that Poo-Poo found led them to something they wished they had never seen.

CHAPTER 3

THE COLOR OF CHEETOS

With his nose raised slightly in the air, Poo-Poo led the way to the house emitting the strongest and most delicious aroma. Scampering along as low as they could, Stick Dog, Mutt, Karen, and Stripes followed him.

It was a small, red brick home with white shutters and two oak trees in the front yard. The trees had lost only a few of their leaves. The dogs settled in behind the trunk of the biggest tree.

As Stick Dog surveyed their surroundings and eyeballed the house, the others recovered a bit from their long run through the forest.

"Look at that color," Mutt said as he stared up at the big oak's branches and leaves.

"What color?" asked Karen, lifting her head to see where Mutt was looking.

"The color of the tree leaves," Mutt answered. There was great sensitivity in his

voice. He almost sighed as he spoke. "It's
a combination of colors, I think. Not quite
orange. But not quite yellow either. Sort of
golden, but not completely."

A quiet autumn wind blew through the yard
then, rustling the leaves a bit.

Mutt took a gasp of air as the leaves began
to move. When they did, the last sunshine
of the day darted in and out of the leaves,
creating skinny streams of light that flashed
and then disappeared through the tree.
"Look at that," Mutt whispered. "Just
amazing. It's like the light and the leaves
are dancing. And when that unknown color
is combined with the sunlight, it's almost
magical."

Karen listened to all of this and looked up at

the leaves and the streams of light. "I think I know, Mutt," she said matter-of-factly.

Mutt was still and quiet; his head remained pointed up toward the furthermost reaches of the oak tree. After a moment, he whispered, "Know what?"

"I think I know what that color is," Karen said. She was not whispering. "I've seen it before."

"Tell me," sighed Mutt. "Tell me where you've seen it before."

"Cheetos," answered Karen. "Crunchy Cheetos. That's the color, all right."

Mutt dropped his head. "Cheetos?"

"Yeah, that's right," Karen said. "Crunchy Cheetos. I just found a few at my favorite garbage can at Picasso Park a couple of days ago. That color up in the tree? It's Cheetos. Crunchy Cheetos."

"You're seriously comparing this moment and this color to a snack?"

"It's not just any snack, Mutt," said Karen, beginning to defend her position. "It's Crunchy Cheetos. They're both colorful and delicious."

Mutt lowered his eyes and looked at the ground. He began to shake his head slowly back and forth.

Karen wanted to make sure that Mutt understood. She said, "Now, I'm not talking about the puffy kind. Those are not quite as delicious and not quite as colorful. I'm talking about the crispy ones with the wrinkles."

Mutt lifted his head.

When he did, Karen decided a little physical explanation might help him understand. She brought her front left paw to her mouth and pretended to hold a Crunchy Cheeto. Then she chomped her teeth together several times, demonstrating the crunchiness of the imaginary Cheeto. Next, Karen looked up into the tree and pointed toward the rustling leaves and sunlight, and then chomped some more and pointed at her mouth. Finally, she said, "Get it?"

Mutt simply nodded and glanced back toward the top of the tree. The wind had settled now, the sun had set, and the leaves looked more brown than anything.

It was just then that Stick Dog said, "Let's see if we can get a peek into that open window. That must be where the smell is coming from. It's probably the kitchen."

"Maybe they have some Crunchy Cheetos

in there," Karen said. "All of a sudden, I'm really in the mood for Crunchy Cheetos."

"Umm, maybe," Stick Dog said as he looked at the open window. "That's kind of a tall windowsill. See the one with the flowerpot on it? Stripes, I think you're the tallest on your hind legs. Can you run over there and prop yourself up on the window to try to see inside? Just be careful not to knock over that flowerpot."

Stripes nodded and stretched her front and back legs a bit, readying to sprint across the lawn.

"Ahem," said Karen in a low voice.

Stick Dog turned to her. "What is it, Karen?"

Karen did not answer. She simply looked at the scattered oak leaves on the ground as her tail drooped.

"Come on," said Stick Dog. "I can tell something is bothering you."

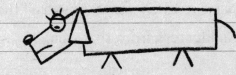

"It's just I never get considered for the 'big dog' parts of our plans," she said quietly, tail still drooping. "I'm tired of being disappointed all the time. Maybe you four *giants* could give me a chance at one of the big dog jobs, that's all."

Stick Dog came a step closer.

"We all have a role to play in our quests for delicious treats and scraps, Karen," Stick Dog said. "No one's job is more or less important."

She nodded a little but didn't seem very convinced.

"Look," Stick Dog said, "think back to that day when we retrieved all those frankfurters from that cart."

Poo-Poo, Stripes, and Mutt all nodded and remembered that glorious day fondly. Even Karen seemed to perk up a little.

"That was a great day, wasn't it?" asked Stick Dog.

"And a great meal," added Mutt, trying to help.

Karen nodded again.

"Well, you're the one who got trapped in the laundry basket. Remember?" Stick Dog asked. "None of *us* are small enough to get inside a basket like that."

"Maybe so," said Karen, a little more loudly.

"And none of us could have jumped out of a second-story window after they got trapped inside the house, right?" Stick Dog asked. "We would have all broken our legs. Not you though. You were able to jump right out so we could catch you and everything. If I remember correctly, you were like a beautiful, majestic bird flying out of that window and landing so gracefully right in the middle of that sheet."

"Yeah, I guess so," Karen said. Stick Dog noticed that her tail had risen a good bit.

"And when we all got stacked up behind that sheet, who was on top?"

Karen smiled. "I don't remember."

"Yes, you do," Stick Dog said. "Who was it? Was it Mutt the giant? Was it Poo-Poo the huge beast? Was it Stripes the enormous? Was it big, old, fatty-fat me?"

Now Karen's tail was wagging. "No," she laughed.

"Who was it?" Stick Dog asked a final time.

"It was me," Karen said. Her tail was wagging like mad now and slapped Poo-Poo in the knee three times every second.

"Now, come on," Stick Dog said with both

joy and a smidgen of authority in his voice. "Let's do this thing. Stripes, let's see what we're up against. Go for it."

With that, Stripes was off. She dashed from behind the tree, across the lawn, and came skidding up to the window. The grass was a little wet and slick and Stripes slid past the window and smashed into a row of hedges.

She untangled herself quickly, regained her balance, and stretched her forepaws up to the windowsill to look inside. When she did, she bashed her head into the little flowerpot and it came crashing to the ground. She dropped instantly back down and sprinted back. Stripes ran as fast as anyone had ever seen. She had a look of pure terror on her face. Her eyes bulged, her lips were drawn back, and her head seemed to be vibrating—almost shaking—as she ran back toward the oak tree.

You would think, perhaps, that she ran so fast because she had been seen by a human. Or maybe because the flowerpot made such a big noise. Or maybe she ran because a human was coming to investigate the sound.

None of those reasons was true.

CHAPTER 4

WHAT STRIPES SAW

When Stripes neared the oak tree where Stick Dog, Mutt, Poo-Poo, and Karen were still situated, she did not break stride. She did not slow down. She did not stop.

She passed them and screamed, "Run for your lives!"

Now, when someone sprints past you screaming, "Run for your lives!" it is typically not a good time to pour yourself

a lemonade and consider what might be
pursuing the person who just ran past you.

No.

When someone rockets past you screaming,
"Run for your lives!" it is, in fact, time for
you to run for your life too.

And that's just what the other dogs did.
They ran as fast as they could after Stripes.
They didn't look for any humans. They didn't
look for any eating opportunities. They even
passed a garbage bag that had clearly been
ripped open recently by a raccoon. They
didn't even give it a sniff. They simply ran.
And ran fast.

Stripes streaked to another house across
the street. She ran up the driveway, across

the side lawn, and tumbled to a stop behind
a short section of white picket fence
covered with grapevines in the side yard.
She stopped and stooped behind the fence
to watch her friends race up the driveway.
She heaved and panted to catch her breath
as they barreled across the lawn to join her.

While the others tried to
catch their breath too, Stripes
attempted to explain between
gasps. "You . . . won't believe . . . what
was . . . in . . . that . . . house," she began.

The others, all huffing and panting

themselves, stared at Stripes, waiting for more explanation.

Stripes trembled and shook her head quickly. "You just . . . won't . . . believe it."

"Humans?" Stick Dog asked. "Did they see you?"

Stripes shook her head.

"A dogcatcher?" asked Mutt.

Stripes shook her head.

"An empty kitchen with no food at all?" Poo-Poo asked desperately.

Again, Stripes shook her head no.

Karen asked the final question.

"Do you guys see any grapes on these vines on this fence?" She panted a little more and then added, "I really like grapes. Not as much as barbecue potato chips or Crunchy Cheetos, mind you.
But still quite a bit."

Stick Dog turned his head to look at Karen. "Umm, no, Karen. I don't think there are any grapes left on these vines. It's a little late in the season. And we kind of have an emergency situa—"

Karen interrupted him. "What about raisins?" she asked. "Maybe there are some raisins. I'm not a big fan, but I'm really hungry. And when grapes get old and dried out, they turn into raisins. So, it only makes sense that there might be some raisins in here."

Karen began poking her dachshund nose through the vines, searching for raisins.

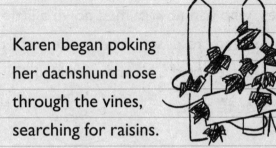

Stick Dog chose to turn back to Stripes. "What was it? What did you see back there?"

Before Stripes could answer, Karen spoke again while she searched through the vines. "Raisins are not as good as grapes and certainly not as good as Crunchy Cheetos. Still, I am pretty darn hungry—and raisins would do in a pinch."

She then buried her entire head in the grapevine brambles to search.

Everyone else's attention focused on Stripes, who had now calmed down a little and was ready to describe what she had seen. She trembled a bit and mumbled, "I saw . . . I saw . . ."

She couldn't get any more words out.

Stick Dog tried to calm her down. He said, "Take a deep breath."

Stripes inhaled deeply.

Stick Dog and the others waited.

Stripes just stood there. She didn't say a word.

And she didn't exhale. Her cheeks were all puffed out.

Stick Dog quickly realized what was happening. "Go ahead and let the air out, Stripes."

Stripes breathed out a great *GUSH* of air.

"I don't know how much longer I could have held that in!" she exclaimed and then panted a few times. "Why did you want me to hold my breath like that, Stick Dog?"

"I just wanted you to breathe deeply and relax," replied Stick Dog. "You know, to calm down so you could tell us what you saw."

"What I saw?"

"Through that kitchen window," Stick Dog reminded.

"Oh, right," Stripes answered, and began to tremble again.

Stick Dog recognized that the whole breathing thing had not worked at all. He took a different route. He asked quickly and directly, "What did you see?"

To Stick Dog's satisfaction, Stripes answered quickly and directly.

She said, "I saw two witches!"

Nobody responded for several seconds.

Finally, Stick Dog asked, "Witches?"

"Witches," Stripes repeated and nodded. "Two of them."

Stick Dog smiled.
And when he did, Mutt and Poo-Poo
seemed to relax a little. They were clearly
happy to see that Stick Dog was relieved.
It made them feel less scared immediately.

Just then Karen called,
"Hey, guys!"

"In a minute, Karen,"
Stick Dog answered.

He was still smiling a little. He knew there were no such things as witches. He didn't know what Stripes had seen through that window, but Stick Dog guessed that her eyesight was blurry from running so fast and bonking her head into the flowerpot on the windowsill. "I need to talk to Stripes here for a minute."

"Oh, sorry," Karen said. She continued to nudge her nose among the grapevines. "It's probably not important anyway. I'll tell you later."

With that, Stick Dog turned to Stripes again. In a calm voice, he said, "I'm not sure what you saw. But I'm pretty sure it wasn't a witch."

"You mean two witches," said Stripes.

"Right, right. Two witches," Stick Dog said. "I'm pretty sure you didn't see two witches."

"How can you be so sure?"

"Well, first of all, they don't exist. Nobody has ever seen real witches before."

"I have," Stripes corrected. "Just now."

"Umm, okay," Stick Dog said slowly. "Nobody has ever seen them before because they don't exist. Those are just stories to scare little puppies. You know, make-believe things."

Stripes began to look a little more comfortable. She knew Stick Dog was pretty smart and knew a lot of things. She was beginning to believe—and hope—that he was right. "What do you think I saw then?"

Stick Dog replied, "Well, I think maybe your eyesight was a little fuzzy or something. You hit your head into that flowerpot pretty good. And I think—"

"Hey, guys?" Karen called again. Her voice was still muffled by the grapevines. She was so deep into the foliage now that the other dogs couldn't even see her head at all.

"Karen, please," Stick Dog said. "Just a second."

"Okay," Karen answered. "Never mind."

But now curiosity had gotten the best of
Mutt and Poo-Poo. They wanted to know
what Karen was up to.

Poo-Poo asked, "Did you find any grapes?"

"No," Karen called back.

"Any raisins?" asked Mutt.

"No," Karen said again.

"Then what's so important?" Poo-Poo asked.

Karen rustled her body through the
grapevines some more, getting even deeper.
Now they couldn't even see her shoulders.
"It's nothing," Karen answered. You could
tell there were some vines stuck in her
mouth as she talked. It was kind of mumbly.

"Stick Dog's right. I shouldn't interrupt so often. I need to work on that. I'll wait until he's done."

Everybody—well, everybody but Karen—turned their attention back to Stick Dog. "So I don't know what you saw, Stripes," he said, picking up the conversation again. But his words came more slowly, as if he was distracted by something. "There's no such—"

And then he stopped completely.

He turned to the white picket fence and searched for Karen. She was very difficult to spot. Only her left hind leg and thin dachshund tail protruded from the tangle of vines and yellowing leaves.

"Karen, could you come out here, please?" he called.

Karen backed out, shook some twigs and leaves from her coat, and took a single quick step toward them all. "Yes, Stick Dog?" she said. "What can I do for you?"

Stick Dog smiled. "There's obviously something on your mind and I'd like to know what it is," he answered. "I've gotten so curious about it. I just want to know so I can get back to convincing Stripes that there are no such things as witches. Then we can all calm down and return to that house and see if we can find something to eat."

"Oh, I see," Karen said, and nodded.

"So, what is it?" Stick Dog asked. "What is it that you wanted to tell us?"

Karen looked over her shoulder through the fence and then back to Stick Dog. "I just thought you'd like to know there are two

witches crossing the

street and coming this

way. That's all."

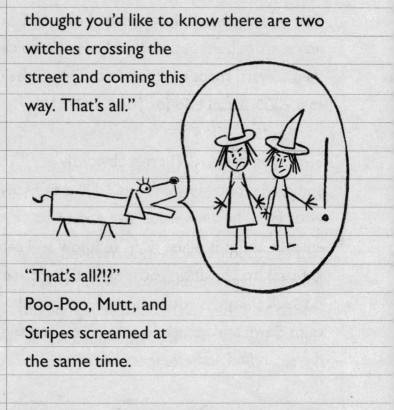

"That's all?!?"
Poo-Poo, Mutt, and
Stripes screamed at
the same time.

"Mm-hmm, that's all," Karen said casually.

Then she added almost as an afterthought,

"Well, except for the fact that they're both

carrying round orange human heads with

them."

Stick Dog, Stripes, Mutt, and Poo-Poo stood utterly still and silent.

For three seconds.

Then they all began moving in very different ways.

Stripes stood in place—but shivered all over. Her legs wobbled so severely that it looked as if they might collapse completely. "Iknewitlknewitlknewit," she muttered as she shook.

Mutt began to shake too—but he seemed to have a purpose to his movement. After a few seconds, he looked all around on the ground at the things that fell from his fur. It was as if he was seeking something to use—a weapon of some sort perhaps—to fend off the approaching witches. All that fell out, however, were two sticks, an old pencil, and one-third of a hard rubber Frisbee. After finding nothing to defend himself and his friends, he leaned his head down to the ground, picked up the piece of Frisbee in his mouth, and began chewing on its edges. This seemed to bring him a good deal of comfort.

Poo-Poo began hopping up and down and jerked his head left and right.

He, like Stripes, muttered something over and over again. He said quickly, "StickDogStickDogStickDog."

Karen ducked her head back into the grapevines and said, "There has to be one grape left in here somewhere."

Stick Dog moved rapidly too. He leaped and slid to the white picket fence. He brushed aside some of the vines to get a clearer view of the driveway and street through the fence slats.

He couldn't believe his eyes.

CHAPTER 5

STEW INGREDIENTS

"It's definitely two witches," Stick Dog
said urgently. He watched as they crossed
the street and headed in their direction.
"Coming this way!"

Stick Dog quickly scanned their
surroundings. There wasn't much there.
This particular house had only a lawn and

no trees or play equipment to hide behind.
Only the single section of picket fence
provided any cover. And with its slatted
openings and fading grapevines, Stick Dog
knew it was a bad hiding place for five
dogs—especially with Karen digging through
the vines and shaking everything.

There was a car parked in the driveway and
Stick Dog made a quick decision. "Everybody
on your bellies," he whispered. "We're going
under that car."

Poo-Poo snapped his head
around quickly. "Under a car?! No way!
Too dangerous. You only go under cars for
emergency situations."

Stripes had fallen out of her frozen position and dropped to her belly immediately. "There are two witches coming after us!" she whispered. "This IS an emergency situation!"

"Right, right," Poo-Poo said as if he just remembered. He quickly dropped to his belly as well.

Stick Dog pulled Karen from the grapevines and led the way to the dark blue station wagon parked short of the garage. The car itself blocked the view of the two witches as they came up the long driveway, and the five dogs bunched themselves underneath it.

Now, we need to stop here just for a minute. You know that hiding under cars is dangerous, right? I mean, do I really need to say that? There are way better—and less dangerous—hiding places around the house. Want to know my favorite hiding place— you know, for a game of hide-and-seek or at homework time? Do you?

It's out in the middle of the yard. I stand really still and put my arms out real crooked-like.

I pretend to be a tree.

For real.

Works almost every time.

For instance, it always works at homework time. I run out to the backyard, pretend to be a tree, and—wah-lah!—homework is delayed. I know it works because I see my parents come to the patio door and stare right at me out in the backyard. They have this weird, puzzled expression on their faces. And I know exactly what they're thinking. They're thinking: "Jeez, we don't remember planting a tree in that spot before."

Smart, hunh?

Eventually, though, my arms get tired and I have to  come inside and do my homework. You should try it though.

So, hiding under cars is a bad idea.

Pretending to be a tree is an excellent idea.

Got it?

Okay, back we go.

"It's not too bad under here," Karen commented. She was the only one short enough to fit comfortably beneath the car. She even got up on her paws once, did a complete circle, and plopped down again in the exact same position.

"Don't get too comfortable," Poo-Poo said, and struggled to look back over his shoulder at Karen. "Because in a couple of minutes, we'll be captured by two witches."

"What will they do to us?" asked Mutt.

Poo-Poo seemed to know about such things and answered, "The witches will certainly put us in a pot with vegetables and poison and bugs and stuff. We'll be boiled into some kind of stew for them to feed to all their witch friends."

"What kind of vegetables, Poo-Poo?" asked Karen.

"What?!"

"What kind of vegetables do you think

they'll use?" Karen asked again. "I love vegetables. Potatoes, carrots, broccoli. I really love carrots. And since I'm going to be in that pot, maybe I could get a few."

"Are you crazy? How can you even think about that?"

"I'm hungry. And, you know, I really like vegetables."

"You're going to be *in* the pot, Karen!" Poo-Poo exclaimed. He talked fast, but still whispered. It was obvious he couldn't believe what he heard.

"Shh!" said Stick Dog. "They're starting to walk up the driveway."

"They must be using their evil witch noses to follow our path," said Poo-Poo, snapping his head back around to confirm that the witches were, in fact, coming their way. After hitting his head on the muffler, he said, "It's all over."

"Hey, Poo-Poo?" asked Mutt.

"Yes?"

"I was wondering about these bugs you were talking about," he said. "You know, the ones that boil in the witch's pot with us?"

"What about them?"

"What kind of bugs will they be? Any idea?"

Even though Poo-Poo's eyes were fixed on the driveway, he answered Mutt. "I don't know."

"Will there be any green ones with blue wings?" asked Mutt sincerely.

"I don't know."

"I hope so," Mutt replied. He waited to see

if anyone would ask him why he hoped so, but nobody did. And after a few seconds he said, "Whenever I hung my head out of the mail truck with my former owner, Gary, I always got bugs in my teeth. And every now and then I would get this little green one with blue wings. Man, that was good eating. I sure hope there are some of those tasty little dudes when I'm in the pot being boiled into a stew."

Poo-Poo twisted his head around to look at Mutt to see if he was serious. He knew he was when Mutt continued speaking.

"Have I ever told you how great it is to ride in a car?" he asked. And now his words and speech pattern began to gain momentum. He got excited with the memory. "The wind blows back your fur and it cools you off instantly. But the best things are the bugs! Lots of delicious ones can fly into your mouth. Now, you can get some bad ones too. It's kind of random. But that's just the price you pay to get some of those delicious buggy morsels! That's why I asked about the little green ones with blue wings, Poo-Poo. If there are some of those floating around to eat when I'm boiled in a witch's stew, I don't think that would be so bad."

"You don't?" asked Poo-Poo.

Mutt shook his head. "Let me tell you, those little green guys are like gourmet bugs, man."

The witches were now halfway up the

driveway. And Stick Dog whispered, "Shh! Now! They're close!"

This got Mutt's attention. He quieted down instantly but did begin to lick his lips a lot.

"What do we do, Stick Dog?" Stripes asked quickly. "What do we do?"

"Hold still."

Stick Dog knew exactly how dangerous this situation was. And he was pretty sure he knew what was going to happen. He had never thought witches were real, but he now knew he was wrong. There was, after all, real live evidence getting closer and closer. Stick Dog figured one very simple thing was going to happen—and he would be ready.

Those witches would stoop down and reach under the car and grab one of them. When that happened, Stick Dog figured, there would be a slim chance the remaining four dogs could escape from the other side of the car.

The witches were nine steps away.

"Listen," Stick Dog whispered over his shoulder to the others. There was absolute seriousness in his voice. "These witches are going to reach under here and try to grab one of us."

At hearing this, the other dogs scooted
back as best they could.

Stick Dog did the opposite thing. He inched
out to the edge of the car—and closer to
the witches.

The witches were seven steps away.

"Keep your eyes wide open and stay alert,"
he instructed quickly. "When you see them
grab me, you guys run out the other side as

fast as you can. Run in different directions.
Find your way back to my pipe. And stay
there until you're all back together."

"Why?" Stripes whispered.

"So you can take care of each other," Stick
Dog answered quietly.

The witches were five steps away.

Stick Dog scooted
out more. Now
his nose poked
out from beneath
the rear bumper.

"Don't do it," Poo-Poo whispered, realizing
what Stick Dog had planned. "Don't let them
grab you."

"No, Stick Dog," Stripes pleaded.

"Just get ready to run," Stick Dog replied. His mind was made up.

The witches were three steps away.

"Stick Dog?" Karen asked in a voice that was way more serious than she usually used.

"Yes?"

"Could you try to bring back some vegetables?" she asked. "I'm really hungry."

"And maybe some bugs?" Mutt added.

The witches were one step away.

CHAPTER 6

CANDY IS DANDY

Guess what?

The witches didn't stop. They didn't reach under the car and grab Stick Dog. They didn't yank him out and boil him in a stew.

Not at all.

Do you know what they did?

They walked by.

That's it.

And Stick Dog, once he was sure they were well past their hiding spot beneath the station wagon, exhaled. His shoulders dropped back down into a comfortable position—well, as comfortable as he could get them when scrunched under a car.

He turned his head to look at the others.

All four dogs were huddled tightly together with their paws covering their eyes.

"Guys?" Stick Dog asked.

Nobody budged.

"You guys?"

There was not a single movement from Poo-Poo, Stripes, Mutt, or Karen.

"You were supposed to have your eyes wide open, remember?" Stick Dog said, and smiled. "So you could see the exact moment they grabbed me—and then sprint in the opposite direction. Remember?"

Nobody spoke or moved.

"It's safe now," he said. "You can open your eyes."

Finally, Karen answered him. "H-how do w-we know you're not using w-witch magic to change your voice and sound like Stick Dog?"

"Open your eyes and you can see me."

They uncovered their eyes and opened them just barely.

"You c-could have transformed yourself from a w-witch into S-S-Stick Dog to t-trick us," Mutt said, and shook his head. "Or you m-m-might be the g-ghost of Stick Dog."

"It's me," Stick Dog said. He tried to think of a way to convince them when his body made a sound.

Do you know what it was?

It was his stomach.

It grumbled.

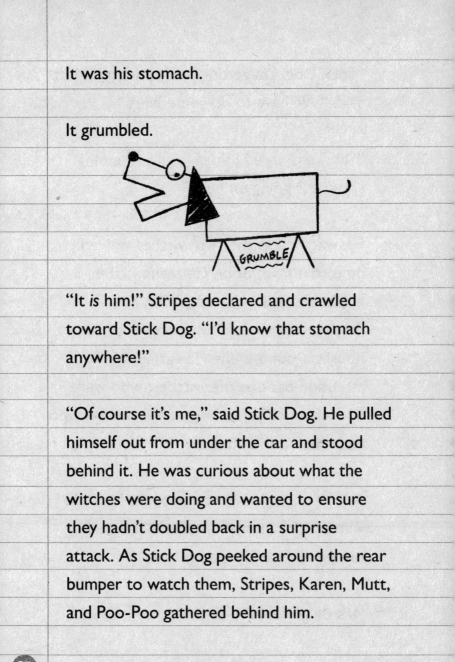

"It *is* him!" Stripes declared and crawled toward Stick Dog. "I'd know that stomach anywhere!"

"Of course it's me," said Stick Dog. He pulled himself out from under the car and stood behind it. He was curious about what the witches were doing and wanted to ensure they hadn't doubled back in a surprise attack. As Stick Dog peeked around the rear bumper to watch them, Stripes, Karen, Mutt, and Poo-Poo gathered behind him.

"Stick Dog, I'm getting really hungry," Mutt said. "We have to do something."

"Shh," answered Stick Dog. "Something strange is going on here."

He watched as the two witches walked up to the front door. He scanned the neighborhood—the sidewalks, the driveways, and the front porches of several houses around them. He turned his attention back to the witches, who were now chanting something to the person who had opened the door.

A look of realization came to his face. He watched for another moment and then turned to face his friends.

"It's okay. Nothing to be scared of," Stick

Dog whispered, and smiled at them. "Back
to the fence with the grapevine. We need to
make a plan."

When they got to this safer and more
familiar location, Poo-Poo, Mutt, and Stripes
came up close to Stick Dog to hear about
what he had observed. Karen did not.
She meandered back to the grapevines
intertwined in the slats of the white picket
fence.

"Karen, what are you doing?" Stick Dog
asked. "You already searched through there,
remember? There weren't any grapes. Or
raisins."

She looked at Stick Dog and simply
answered, "Maybe some have grown since
I was here last."

"Umm," Stick Dog said, and paused. And then he just said, "Okay."

As Karen re-submerged herself in another fruitless search for grapes, Stick Dog addressed only Stripes, Poo-Poo, and Mutt.

"Look, you guys," he began to explain. "I'm starting to think those witches aren't real. I think they might just be wearing costumes.

And there are other humans coming out of their houses wearing costumes too. Most of them are little humans, but there are some big ones too. Only the little ones are dressed up in strange ways."

Poo-Poo, Stripes, and Mutt scanned the neighborhood. Sure enough, there were nearly a dozen small humans walking around on sidewalks and driveways and standing on front porches. None of them were dressed in regular clothes. There were scary ones—the witches, of course, but also some ghosts and a mummy. And there were others that seemed not as scary—like an astronaut, a cowboy, and a princess.

Under normal circumstances, these strangely dressed humans would have confused and frightened them all terribly.

But there was an inflection in Stick Dog's voice that Stripes, Poo-Poo, and Mutt recognized. He was solving a puzzle. And they knew if he could solve the puzzle, then there was a good chance the reward might be something to eat.

"I have a theory about what might be going—" Stick Dog began, but he had to stop. That's because Poo-Poo had something vital to say.

"No need to explain things, Stick Dog," Poo-Poo said with total confidence. "I've already figured it all out. I know everything."

"You do?" asked Mutt, clearly impressed. "Wow. Everything is a lot."

"That's right," Poo-Poo confirmed

confidently. "Go ahead. Ask me anything."

Mutt and Stripes seemed to like the idea of this challenge, relishing an opportunity to stump Poo-Poo. After a few moments of consideration, Mutt asked the first question.

"Can you name three of the five planets in the solar system?"

Poo-Poo tilted his head for a brief moment and then answered, "Wyoming, Orange Ball, and Betty."

WYOMING

BETTY

ORANGE BALL

Mutt was obviously surprised. "Impressive," he whispered.

Stripes took her turn next. "What number comes between three and five?"

Poo-Poo rubbed his chin, bit his lower lip, and tapped his front left paw against the grass several times. This all took twenty or thirty seconds. He didn't seem totally confident in his answer, but he did give it. He said, "Seven."

"Whoa," Stripes said. "You really do know all the right answers."

"Well," he said in an attempt at modesty. "I am Poo-Poo, after all."

"So, umm, seven comes between three and

five?" Stick Dog asked. "I guess I didn't know that."

Poo-Poo gave Stick Dog a sympathetic glance and said, "You're probably just not as good a counter as me."

2, 0, 1, 8, 3, 7, 5, 4...

"I guess not," Stick Dog said, and smiled a bit. He pointed out to the neighborhood then and asked, "How do you explain all these strange humans here tonight? The witches, the astronaut, and the princess, for instance. What are they doing out here?"

Poo-Poo considered this for several ponderous seconds.

"Well?" Stick Dog asked.

"It's quite obvious, actually," Poo-Poo said now that he was pressed for an answer. "The astronaut was flying his spaceship when it crashed into the princess's castle. His spaceship is now broken, but he needs to get to Planet Betty to complete his mission. Witches can fly on brooms. So he and the princess are going to ask the witches if they can borrow their brooms to fly to Planet Betty. Easy-peasy."

"Makes sense," expressed Mutt.

Stripes said, "Totally logical."

"Well, that's one explanation," said Stick Dog. "But I have a slightly different theory."

"What's that?" asked Poo-Poo. He couldn't hide the doubtfulness in his voice.

"I think there's some kind of bizarre human ritual happening," Stick Dog theorized. "It appears the little humans go up to the front door of these houses and shout 'trick or treat.' Then the door opens and the big humans inside drop stuff in their bags or their orange buckets."

"The heads are really buckets?" Poo-Poo asked nervously.

Stick Dog nodded.

"But how do you know it's humans wearing costumes?" asked Mutt. "How do you know the astronaut, princess, and witches are not, you know, an astronaut, princess, and witches?"

"Look at their feet," Stick Dog said, and pointed out into the neighborhood again. "They're all wearing sneakers!"

Stick Dog probably would have explained his theory even further, but it was precisely then that something caught Stick Dog's attention. One witch swung her bucket in a huge arc and a small red packet flew out. It landed softly in the green grass at the edge of the driveway. Stick Dog marked the spot to remember and then turned his head to see Karen rustle her way out of the grapevines.

"Bad news," she muttered. "There's not a single grape in that whole mess."

"You mean none have grown since you last searched?" Stick Dog asked as sincerely as he could muster.

Karen hung her head low and then shook it. She seemed bitterly disappointed with the result of her grape search.

"Karen?" Stick Dog asked. "Can you wait here just a minute? I'm going to go get something."

She nodded but didn't look up.

To Stripes, Poo-Poo, and Mutt, he said, "Stay here. I'll be right back."

With that, Stick Dog inched his way to the picket fence's final post. He looked left and then right and then left again. He saw several humans, but none were very close—and they all seemed preoccupied with the night's festivities. It was also growing darker. Stick Dog thought it was safe enough.

He sprinted about three-quarters of the way down the driveway to the exact spot where that red packet had come flying out of the orange bucket. He sifted through the grass for a few seconds with his paws. Stick Dog heard a crackling sound and saw the shiny red packet reflecting the moonlight. He picked it up and hurried back to his friends.

When Stick Dog reached Mutt, Stripes, Poo-Poo, and Karen, he dropped the red packet on the ground. They looked, pawed, and sniffed at it.

"Let's see what's inside," Stick Dog said. "The witches seemed happy to get this, so it must be okay."

With that, Stick Dog pinned a corner of the packet beneath his front left paw and tore at it with his front right paw. When he did, the red packet ripped open quickly and sprayed several colorful round candies across the ground.

CHAPTER 7

ATTACK OF THE CHERRY PITS

"See these little things?" Stick Dog said, and pointed at a few of the yellow, green, purple, orange, and red balls scattered about on the ground. He pushed a couple around with his paws. They wobbled and rolled around a bit. "These must be candy. I heard the witches talk about it when they passed by."

Poo-Poo sniffed at one of the red candy balls. "It smells funny," he whispered after a couple of long sniffs. "It smells sweet and familiar. Do you think I should taste it, Stick Dog?"

"I think it's safe," Stick Dog said immediately. "I've been watching the little humans who are out tonight. They reach into their sacks and buckets and eat the stuff they grab."

"You're sure?" asked Poo-Poo. He was becoming a little more comfortable with the idea.

"Pretty sure," Stick Dog answered. "But I'll go first if you want me to."

Poo-Poo immediately raised a paw in the air. "That won't be necessary, Stick Dog. I'm not afraid," he said as he leaned down to pick up the red Skittle. "I'm really the expert here, as we all know."

Stick Dog nodded. "Okay, then."

Poo-Poo gripped a tiny red ball with his
lips and lifted it off the ground and into his
mouth. You could tell by the movement
of his jaw and cheeks that he was rolling it
around in his mouth. After several seconds
he bit into it and began to chew.

And chew.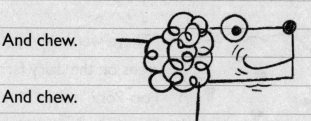

And chew.

And then he smiled and chewed some more.

"Well?" Karen, Mutt, and Stripes all asked at
once.

"This so-called 'candy' is an invigorating
blend of high-fructose corn syrup, sugar, and
fruity flavoring," Poo-Poo announced at the
start of his description. "I taste perfectly

ripe cherries at the front of my palate and a tart but sugary blast against my inner cheeks. This savory and sweet flavor evokes memories from my early days as a puppy on the dairy farm. There was a small orchard there with a few cherry trees."

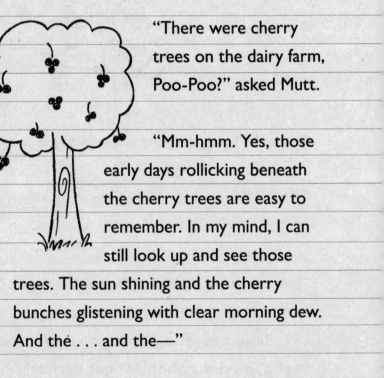

"There were cherry trees on the dairy farm, Poo-Poo?" asked Mutt.

"Mm-hmm. Yes, those early days rollicking beneath the cherry trees are easy to remember. In my mind, I can still look up and see those trees. The sun shining and the cherry bunches glistening with clear morning dew. And the . . . and the—"

Poo-Poo suddenly stopped speaking then. His voice had been calm, almost soothing, until that moment. Then a strange, out-of-place grimace came over his face. And his voice turned harsh and angry. "And the . . . and the . . ."

"And the what, Poo-Poo?" asked Mutt. The others were curious too. The stark change in Poo-Poo's expression and voice had caught their full attention.

"And the SQUIRRELS! That's what!" Poo-Poo screamed. His eyes were wide and menacing as he remembered. "I can see those nasty tail-shakers up in those cherry trees! They're up in those trees with their puffy tails and snickering mouths. Chitter-chatter-chitter! Look at us! We can have all the cherries we want! We can bounce from branch to branch. Aren't we SO special?! YOU have to wait for the cherries to fall! But WE can have cherries whenever we want! We can shove them into our chubby cheeks anytime! Erggh! Those darn squirrels! Oh, I can't stand those sniveling chatterboxes!!!"

"Poo-Poo?" Stick Dog said calmly.

Poo-Poo didn't hear him.

"They got all the perfectly ripe cherries! Those rotten, fluffy-tailed varmints!" Poo-Poo snarled. "All I got was the leftovers that fell to the ground. And the pits! They shot cherry pits at me like machine gun fire!"

"Poo-Poo?" Stick Dog said calmly, but louder.

"Rat-a-tat-tat! Rat-a-tat-tat! Watch out for cherry pits! Incoming cherry pits!" Poo-Poo was practically screaming. He was dodging his head up and down, left and right to avoid the imaginary cherry pit bombardment. "Rat-a-tat-tat!"

"Poo-Poo!" Stick Dog said—even louder.

This finally got Poo-Poo's attention. It wasn't very often, after all, that Stick Dog raised his voice. Poo-Poo turned his head immediately to face him.

"We're not at the dairy farm," Stick Dog said. His tone was calm but firm. "You're with your friends now. Besides you proved your superiority to squirrels on that glorious day when we discovered donuts. Remember? And those squirrels back on the dairy farm?"

"Yes?" Poo-Poo snarled, conjuring the memory again. "What about those cherry-pit-dropping villains?"

"I bet they've never tasted candy like you just did," Stick Dog continued. "If they could see you right now, chewing on sweet, delicious candy—they would be SO jealous. Wouldn't they?"

This thought turned Poo-Poo's snarl into a smile instantly.

"I bet they've never tasted candy before in their lives!" Poo-Poo exclaimed.

"Or hamburgers," added Mutt.

"Or frankfurters," Stripes chimed in.

"Or pizza," added Karen.

"Or ice cream," said Stick Dog.

This cooled off Poo-Poo completely. He waved at the air above his head where he had imagined those cherry trees from his puppyhood had been. "Keep your cherries, you furry-faced fuzz-buckets," he whispered up at the empty space. Now satisfied, Poo-Poo dropped his head and looked toward Stick Dog.

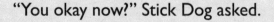

"You okay now?" Stick Dog asked.

"I'm cool as a cucumber," replied Poo-Poo.

"I lo-o-o-ve cucumbers," Karen moaned instantly. "Even more than grapes."

"We'll look for cucumbers some other time," said Stick Dog quickly. He didn't want Karen distracted from their current mission. "But right now, we're after some more of this candy."

"How are we going to get some?" Karen asked, having already forgotten about cucumbers entirely.

"We'll need a plan," Stick Dog said.

They shared, ate—and LOVED—the rest of the candy. And they contemplated possible ways to snatch some more.

Chapter 8

FLUFFORABLE

"I know how to do it," Mutt said.

"Me too!" Stripes, Karen, and Poo-Poo all said at exactly the same time.

Stick Dog leaned back against the picket fence to get more comfortable. He had the distinct feeling this might take some time. He said, "Okay, Mutt, you first. Let's hear your plan for snatching some candy."

But Mutt didn't answer. Instead, he crossed his eyes and pulled his mouth to one side. Then he made kind of a deep gurgling sound from the back of his throat.

"Are you okay?" Stick Dog asked.

Mutt nodded and kept contorting his facial features in strange ways.

"You sure you're not choking?" Stripes asked.

Mutt nodded again. He lifted his shoulders higher, stuck his head forward, and squinted his eyes. Again, he made that odd, deep gurgling sound.

"Are you going to barf or something?" asked Karen.

Mutt shook his head but continued to make the face—and make the sound.

He tilted his head, lifted the left side of his lip to expose some teeth, and leaned down as if he was about to charge the four others.

"Is this a guessing game?" asked Poo-Poo.

Mutt shook his head.

Finally, Stick Dog said, "Stop whatever it is you're doing, Mutt. Just for a minute. What are you trying to show us?"

Mutt relaxed his face and body. "I'm demonstrating my plan," he began to explain. "See, I'm going to look real mean and growl and—"

"*That* was a growl?!" Poo-Poo interrupted and snickered. "Dude. You have *got* to work on your growl. That's the funniest growl I've ever heard."

Mutt chose to ignore the comment and continued to explain his plan. "I'm going to look real mean and growl at those little humans or at the people at the door. When they see—"

But Poo-Poo couldn't help himself and interrupted again. "I mean, that so-called 'growl' of yours, Mutt. Jeez. No offense, but not too scary—you know what I mean? I thought you were going to sneeze or something. Or maybe you ate a bad bug or something. But growling? I wouldn't have guessed that was growling in a million years."

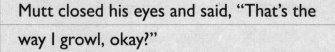

Mutt closed his eyes and said, "That's the way I growl, okay?"

Poo-Poo nodded. "Sure, it's okay. To each his own. No problem. I'm just saying if that's the growl you're going to use, you might want to come up with a different plan."

Mutt opened his eyes and turned to Stick Dog—and Stick Dog only. "I look real mean and growl, see? Then the little humans in the costumes drop their candy and run away. When they do, we grab it and go back to your pipe for a sweet and tasty feast."

Stick Dog nodded his head in understanding. "I see. Yes, yes. There's quite a lot of merit in your strategy."

Mutt glanced over at Poo-Poo, who shook his head, giggled, and whispered to himself. "I mean, it was more like a kitten purring or something."

Stick Dog said, "I like it. I really do. It's just hard for me to picture you looking mean, Mutt. And, if you think about it, that's really a good thing. Someone like you just can't

fake being mean. You're just too handsome.
You're too fluffy. You're too adorable."

"You're fluffy and adorable," repeated
Karen, in an attempt to help.
"You're flufforable."

MR. FLUFFORABLE

"Karen's right," Stick Dog
said, and smiled. "You're
flufforable."

Mutt considered this for a moment. "So,
what you're saying is that I'm *too* good-
looking to be able to pull off this plan?"

Stick Dog nodded.

"Hmm," Mutt said, and then thought about
it for just a second or two more. "I can live
with that."

Stick Dog turned to Poo-Poo then. "What do you have for us?"

"We're going to need a bag," Poo-Poo began. "It needs to be big enough for all of us to fit into."

"A garbage bag might work," said Karen. "Those are pretty big."

Poo-Poo nodded. "Good suggestion."

"I don't know," said Stick Dog. "I don't think a garbage bag is strong enough to hold all five of us. Those things tear pretty easily. Heck, we tear into them all the time looking for food. They're just not that strong."

"Don't worry about it. In my plan, the bag only needs to hold four of us anyway," Poo-

Poo said, dismissing this potential obstacle. He inhaled and began pacing. Then he stopped suddenly as if the rest of his plan had instantly crystallized in his mind. "We're all going to climb into the bag—except for you, Stick Dog. So Stripes, Mutt, Karen, and I all climb into the bag. Then you carry us all around the neighborhood."

Stick Dog didn't mention he thought it would be impossible to carry them all by himself in a bag that they would probably never be able to find. Instead, he asked, "What then?"

In rapid succession, Poo-Poo provided the other steps of his plan. "We stop at each house just like the little humans are doing. You ring the bell. The large humans open the door and see you there with a big bag like everybody else. Now, they're going to be waiting for you to say 'trick or treat,' right?"

"Right," Stick Dog answered slowly.

"But you don't speak human language, right?"

"Right," Stick Dog answered even more slowly.

"So that's when you start coughing a lot," Poo-Poo explained. "That way they won't notice that you can't speak human language. You'll also want to shake your head violently while you're coughing. That way they won't see your face very well. While you're having

a coughing attack, they'll see your bag and
start dropping candy into it."

"Hey, Poo-Poo,"
Karen interrupted.

"Yes?"

"I just wanted to say that I love your plan
so far."

"Thanks. I assumed you would love it
because great plans like this are always
accepted and adored by those who hear
them," Poo-Poo said, and returned to the
task at hand. "The real genius part of the
plan occurs while Stick Dog is coughing up
a storm and the big humans are dropping

candy into the bag."

Stick Dog tilted his head and asked, "You mean there's even more to the plan than me carrying the four of you around the neighborhood in a garbage bag, ringing all the doorbells, the big humans not recognizing that I'm a dog, coughing my head off, and the candy being dropped into the bag?"

"The best is yet to come," Poo-Poo said.

"I can believe that," Stick Dog whispered so quietly that nobody else could hear him.

"The four of us are in the bag when they drop the candy in," Poo-Poo continued with the final details of his strategy. "When they drop it in, we have our mouths open. So they will—Ta-da!—just drop food directly into our mouths. And the food will disappear as we eat it and eat it. They'll glance down in the bag, see that the food is disappearing, and then just pour more and more in. I'd say in a few houses, our stomachs will be bursting!"

Mutt, Karen, and Stripes all nodded enthusiastically as Poo-Poo wrapped up his explanation.

"What about Stick Dog?" Mutt asked.

"Oh, we'll save some stuff in the bottom of the bag for him," Poo-Poo added.

"Thanks, I appreciate that," Stick Dog

said. He paused briefly and tried to think of something to say. He knew the plan would never work for a wide variety of reasons. But he didn't want to say that. Instead, he said, "I'm a bit concerned about how your plan will affect the little humans."

"How so?" asked Poo-Poo.

"Well, they seem really happy and excited to be out here tonight in their costumes and everything," explained Stick Dog. "But if the big humans keep dumping more and more candy into our bag, there won't be any left for the little humans. It doesn't seem right is all."

"You don't think we should get as much food as we can, Stick Dog?" Stripes asked, confused. "That doesn't sound like you."

"No, I would never say that," Stick Dog answered. "But Poo-Poo's excellent plan would empty several houses of all the food they're passing out. What with you guys constantly eating and the big humans dropping more and more into the bag. And it just seems like it's not very nice considering these little humans are out here having such a good time."

Stick Dog turned to Poo-Poo to see if this was working.

"I think I hear what you're saying," Poo-Poo finally said after a moment of thoughtful consideration. "You're saying that my plan is SO perfect that it won't leave anything left for these little humans at all."

"Exactly," Stick Dog encouraged quickly.

"I'm sorry about that, Stick Dog," Poo-Poo said. "But I'm unable to come up with a bad plan, or an average plan, or even a really good plan. My plans are either excellent or nothing."

Stick Dog squeezed his lips together. "I know, Poo-Poo. I know. I'm sorry we can't use it."

"I have a strategy," Karen interrupted. "And I promise it's not too excellent."

CHAPTER 9

Poodlesaurus Rex

"That's terrific," said Stick Dog, happy to leave Poo-Poo's strategy behind. "What is your plan all about?"

"I think we should build a house," Karen said simply.

Even though Stick Dog didn't look forward to an explanation, which was bound to be both complicated and lengthy, he asked politely, "Why?"

"Because houses must *come* with candy,"
Karen said. "Just look around—everyone
who comes out of a house has a bunch of
candy. They're bringing it from inside! So, if
we build a house, then we'll have access to
lots of candy!"

"Makes sense," Stripes said.

Poo-Poo said, "I'm in."

"I'm ready," Mutt agreed. He then began
shaking a little bit. He aimed, obviously, to
dislodge something they could use from
his fur. "I think I have a screwdriver in here
somewhere."

"Great! That would be useful," Karen said.

Mutt's suggestion seemed to prompt Karen

to think of other things she might need. She began looking around. This concerned Stick Dog a great deal. The litany of things necessary to build a house would take a long time to think of and name. He tried to find a way out of this.

Thankfully, Karen herself provided it.

"We're definitely going to need some wooden boards. Maybe we can tear apart this fence with the grapevines all over it," Karen suggested and glanced over at it. When she did, her eyes focused more on the grapevine than the wooden slats. She tilted her head a little sideways. Without turning to him, Karen asked, "Stick Dog, when was the last time I looked in there for grapes?"

"Oh, it's been a while."

"I LOVE grapes!" exclaimed Karen. "I bet some new ones have grown since then!"

And with that, Karen stopped thinking about building a house that came with its own supply of candy and, instead, began pawing through the grapevines again.

Mutt stopped shaking in an attempt to find a screwdriver. He did pick up a short piece of yellow rope that had sprung out from his fur. He plopped down on his belly and began to chew on it with tremendous satisfaction.

It was now Stripes's turn. Stick Dog didn't even need to ask if she had a plan. She just started speaking.

"We're going to go back to one of those glorious food-finding days in our past," Stripes began. "Remember when we got those frankfurters?"

Stripes had to stop then. Poo-Poo was suddenly super-excited.

"Back in time!? Time travel?!" he asked enthusiastically. "Is that what you're talking about?! I'm all for it. Let's do it!"

"No, not time travel," Stripes said. You could tell she didn't like having her food-finding plan interrupted.

"No time travel? That's a bummer," Poo-Poo sighed. But then he got all excited again. "I've always wanted to go back in time! That would be awesome!"

"Where would you travel back to, Poo-Poo?" Karen called as she continued to search for grapes. She was close enough to hear them all.

"Way back to the days when the Earth was ruled by the great Poodlesaurus Rexes," Poo-Poo answered without pausing for a single second. He had obviously thought about this before.

Mutt allowed the ragged piece of yellow rope to drop from his mouth momentarily. He was curious. "What's a Poodlesaurus Rex?"

"Well, there were dinosaurs all over the place fifty or sixty years ago," Poo-Poo began to explain. "And the dinosaurs were all destroyed by the powerful and mighty Poodlesaurus Rexes. We ruled the Earth for months and months after that."

"What do you mean 'we'?" asked Stripes.

"Well, you know, my ancestors if you want to get technical about it," Poo-Poo answered.

"What did they look like?" asked Mutt.

Poo-Poo sat back and stretched his front paws in a giant arc above his head. "Just imagine me twenty times bigger with claws instead of paws."

Nobody said anything. It was difficult to tell if they were believing Poo-Poo's version of natural history—or considering what a Poodlesaurus Rex might actually look like.

"Anyway, that's why I wanted to time travel in Stripes's plan," Poo-Poo concluded. "I wanted to go back and join the ruling class of my Poodlesaurus Rex ancestors."

There was an extended, almost awkward, pause then. Poo-Poo's eyes were blank and distant. It was as if he could see himself twenty times bigger marauding across the great suburban landscape.

Karen poked her head out of the vines and asked, "Do you think there were ever any dachshund-a-saurs?"

Poo-Poo shook his head and grinned. "I don't think so," he said. "That would be pretty silly-looking, let's be honest."

Karen seemed disappointed, but then she saw a ladybug on one of the grapevine leaves and immediately focused on that instead.

And Stick Dog? Well, Stick Dog didn't know what to say at all. He didn't want to ask Poo-Poo any more questions. He didn't want to squash his ideas about time travel and

Poodlesaurus Rexes either. But he did want
to get some more of that candy.

Thankfully, Stripes knew just what to say.

"Yeah. Well, anyway," she said. "Since my
plan *doesn't* involve time travel, maybe I
should just tell you what it *does* involve."

"Great idea!" Stick Dog said immediately and
with a good bit of enthusiasm.

"Like I said," Stripes continued. "We're going
back to one of those great food-finding days
of our past. Remember the frankfurter man
with the cart? What was his name? Was it
Patsy Puffenstuff?"

"No, it was Prickle Pop," Karen called
without ever taking her eyes off the ladybug.

Poo-Poo joined the conversation. "I think it was Piddly-Pants."

"Nope," Mutt chimed in. He coughed a little as he spit the rope from his mouth to speak. Some of the loose threads were stuck in his teeth. "It was Pumpkin-Head."

Stick Dog lowered his head. He stared at the grass between his front paws. He inhaled and exhaled slowly and evenly three times. Upon raising his head after this breathing exercise, he calmly said, "Peter. His name was Peter."

"That's what I meant," said Stripes. "Well, we scared Peter away because he thought he saw a ghost. I think we should do the same kind of thing again—only this time on purpose. We find some sheets, act like ghosts, and everybody out here tonight will run away screaming. They'll drop their bags and buckets! Candy will be scattered everywhere! We'll be eating all night!"

Stick Dog looked over his shoulder toward the street. He considered it very good fortune when he saw three ghosts—three small humans dressed in ghost costumes, that is—several houses away. Stick Dog motioned Stripes to come stand next to him.

"What is it?" Stripes asked as she approached. "Don't you like my plan, Stick Dog?"

"I absolutely love your plan," Stick Dog

answered emphatically. He then pointed at the three ghosts. "It's just that I don't like *when* your plan happens."

Stripes eyed the ghosts. "Why?"

"Because this is the *one* night out of the whole year when humans *won't* be afraid of ghosts." Stick Dog sighed and shook his head. "There are ghosts and witches and other scary things all over the place."

Stripes asked, "So my plan is excellent every night of the year *except* for this one?"

Stick Dog nodded his head.

"So it's not a bad plan? Just bad timing?"

Stick Dog nodded again.

Stripes shrugged her shoulders and sat down. "What can I do?"

Stick Dog was disappointed but not altogether surprised that his friends' plans hadn't worked out. But now that he knew what candy tasted like, he was determined to figure out a way to get some more.

"Let's track the witches," he suggested, and stepped over to the fence. The ladybug had flown away and Karen was deep in the vines again looking for grapes. Stick Dog pulled gently on her left hind leg as he continued. "We know the witches aren't dangerous now. Maybe if we observe their behavior, we'll think of something."

Karen looked up at Stick Dog after she was completely untangled from the vines and back with her friends.

"No grapes," she sighed.

"Maybe next time," Stick Dog said, and smiled. "Come on."

Chapter 10

STUCK

They all lined up single file behind Stick Dog. There was a large gap in the costumed humans going door-to-door, and the dogs were able to catch up with the witches quickly.

Under the deepening darkness of the night, they ducked behind some bushes to watch the witches at their next stop. It was an older house, with a large metal gate that allowed entrance onto the small front porch. The witches pushed the gate open, took a few steps, and then climbed three stairs to stand before the door.

Stick Dog watched every move the witches made and listened to each word spoken. He noted every detail in the candy-fetching process.

After the witches got their candy and the door closed, Stick Dog ducked back into the bushes as far as he could. He didn't want them to see him, but he did listen closely for more clues as they descended the steps and made their way to the next house.

"I love going to Grandma Smith's house every year," one witch said to the other as they passed. They were completely unaware of the dogs hiding in the bushes. "She makes the best caramel apples in the world!"

"I know," said the other witch. "And she's so nice—even though she can't see or hear so well anymore. She thought I was my older sister."

The other witch laughed. "She thought I was my younger *brother*!"

After the witches had gone a safe distance away, Stick Dog pushed his head out into the open air and looked left and right to ensure no other humans were approaching.

When he was certain it was safe, he came
out of the bushes and motioned for Mutt,
Poo-Poo, Stripes, and Karen to follow him.
He nudged the gate forward a bit so they
could all fit through. He moved slowly,
reenacting what the witches had done
a minute earlier in an attempt to learn
something that might help them retrieve the
delicious treats. As he did this, Stick Dog
whispered the whole process to himself and
the others.

Stripes, Poo-Poo, and Mutt all watched
this closely. Karen took a few seconds to
chase her tail. She didn't catch it and quickly
turned her attention to what Stick Dog was
doing as well.

"Let's see," Stick Dog said as he took a few deliberate steps past four flowerpots and up the three front stairs to the porch. "They come up here. Then they press that button by the door."

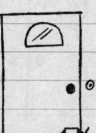 He lifted his head and looked off into the distance to refresh his memory. The sky had grown darker and the first blinking stars had emerged. He lowered his head and continued. "After a few seconds, the door opens and—"

But Stick Dog didn't get a chance to say anything else.

Do you know why?

I'll tell you.

It's because Stripes had reached up with her
front left paw and pressed the button by
the door.

The doorbell button.

Stick Dog, who had
his back to Stripes
when she pressed
the button, spun around when he heard the
loud chime inside. To Stick Dog, it was a
dangerous sound, like an alarm or a siren.
He looked at Stripes, who had dropped
down and now had all four paws on the
cold, concrete front porch.

"What did you just do?!"
asked Stick Dog urgently.

"I pressed the button," said Stripes. She seemed a little surprised that he had asked her.

"Why'd you do that?!" Stick Dog asked. He snapped his head left and right. He didn't know what the chime signaled. But he had an uneasy feeling about it. He and his friends stood exposed out there on that front porch.

"You told me to do it," Stripes answered with a slight quiver in her speech. Her attitude wasn't so casual as before. She sensed the concern coursing through Stick Dog's motions and voice. She saw it on his face. And the others did too. They began to fidget nervously. Poo-Poo backed slowly away from that front door and down the steps.

"No, I didn't," Stick Dog said quickly. He was still snapping his head in all directions to look for oncoming trouble.

"Did too," said Stripes in an attempt to defend herself. "I distinctly heard you say, and I quote, 'Press that button by the door.' Unquote."

Stick Dog shook his head. "I wasn't giving directions. I was just repeating what the small humans did when they—"

But Stick Dog didn't get a chance to finish explaining. That's because two things happened at exactly that moment.

Poo-Poo, still scared and backing down the steps and away from the porch, bumped into the metal gate. It swung effortlessly shut and latched loudly behind them.

It was immediately apparent to all five dogs that they were trapped on the porch now.

"We're stuck!" Karen whispered.

"Uh-oh," said Poo-Poo.

But the gate closing behind them was only the first thing that happened at that precise second.

Do you know what else happened?

The door to the house opened.

Chapter 11

BART, RUTH, RALPH, AND ADAM (AND KAREN)

A large human stood in the doorway of that home and stared at the five dogs in front of her. Her hair was white and wrapped in a circle on top of her head. Stuck sideways into that white ball of hair was a pair of thick eyeglasses.

"Well, well. What do we have here?" the woman said as she squinted down at the dogs. "More trick-or-treaters, I see."

Mutt, Karen, Stripes, and Poo-Poo yanked their heads toward Stick Dog. They stood rock-solid still. They were shocked frozen by the gate clanging shut behind them and the large wooden door opening in front of them.

"What do we do, Stick Dog?" whispered Karen. "We're trapped."

Stick Dog did not have an answer.

This combination of things represented the one great fear in Stick Dog's life. He had always worried they would be discovered—and captured—as a group. He had always known that one or more of his friends might get caught or trapped by a human someday. But Stick Dog also knew he would do everything in his power to rescue any one of them. Now, all five of them were caught in this tight, confined space. He knew their lives as a collective bunch of stray friends was probably over.

"Stick Dog?" Karen whispered quickly again.

But before he could answer, the human in the doorway spoke.

"What are those?" the woman asked.

She squinted her eyes nearly shut and sort of pivoted her head to stare at each dog individually. It was only a few seconds, but  it seemed like forever to Stick Dog. What was the woman thinking? Was she going to call a dogcatcher? Or the police? Or try to catch each of them by herself? Maybe there were other large humans in the house who would come after the dogs too.

She looked at each of them again. She
squinted her eyes even more. "Animal
costumes? Dogs? Is that what you're
supposed to be?"

Because he could think of nothing else to
do, Stick Dog coughed.

"HMM? What's that?" she said loudly. "I
don't have my hearing aids in. WHAT DID
YOU SAY?"

Stick Dog coughed again.

"LOUDER, PLEASE!" she
said, and leaned closer.
"Can't see you either,
dang it! Lost my darn
glasses again."

"Move out of the light a bit," Stick Dog whispered to the others. His confidence grew a little. Maybe they could get out of this somehow. "And stay calm."

The large, old woman turned around in the doorway.

"She's leaving!" Mutt whispered.

"We're safe!" exclaimed Karen in a quiet voice.

"We're still trapped though. Because Poo-Poo hit the gate with his big butt," Stripes whispered.

"My butt's not big!"

"Is too!"

"Is not!"

This might have gone back and forth for a while, but they discovered instantly that the large woman had not left at all. She had simply reached back inside the door to get something. Upon retrieving a tray of caramel-covered apples, she turned back around to face them all. She leaned forward slightly and pushed the tray toward the dogs.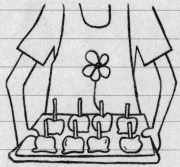

"Well, I can't hear or see very well anymore," the woman said, and smiled genuinely. She had a lovely, friendly face when she smiled. "But I still make the best caramel apples in the neighborhood! Come on and take one! And tell me your names. Nice and loud now."

Stick Dog knew he had to go first. The others were counting on him.

"Bark!" he said.

BARK!

"Well, hello, Bart! It's nice to meet you," the woman said, and pushed the tray in Stick Dog's direction. She turned her head to pick out her next customer. When she did, Stick Dog took one of the sticks in his mouth and lifted an apple from the tray.

Seeing this successful retrieval boosted the others' courage.

"Woof!" Stripes said.

"Ruth! That's my sister's name," the woman said. She grinned widely and lowered the tray down toward Stripes while simultaneously turning to Mutt. "Take a nice big caramel apple, Ruth, dear."

Stripes reached her head above the tray and gripped one of the sticks in her mouth and pulled an apple off.

Mutt barked, "R-Rawf!"

"Ralph! That's a name you don't hear very often anymore. Happy Halloween, Ralph!"

Mutt took an apple.

Poo-Poo stepped forward. He wanted to bark nice and strong like the others. He cleared his throat loudly, "A-hem!"

"Hello, Adam!" the woman said before Poo-Poo could even bark.

Poo-Poo looked a little disappointed that he didn't get a chance to bark. As soon as he got that caramel apple, however, everything was better.

Only Karen remained.

"I guess you're big enough for a caramel apple," the old woman said, and leaned down to lower the tray to Karen. "What's your name, little one?"

Karen didn't like being called "little" like that. And her instinctive response was to growl. And that's just what she did. "Grrrr."

"Yes." The woman nodded good-naturedly. "I know you're a girl."

Just then, and before Karen could make another sound, a booming human voice came out from the house. "Smells like something's burning in the kitchen, Gladys!"

"That's my pumpkin pie!" she exclaimed as her eyes popped open. "I have to go!"

She quickly grabbed an apple off the tray and handed it to Karen. Karen took the stick in her mouth. The human woman didn't notice at all. She had already twisted on her left foot, spun around, and hustled back inside.

She hurriedly put the tray down. Stick Dog could hear a last snippet of the humans' conversation before the door closed.

"Who was that?" the male voice called.

"I'm not sure. Couldn't hear them very well without my hearing aids," the woman

answered. "They were wearing dog
costumes, I think. I couldn't really see them.
Have you seen my glasses?"

"They're on your head!" the man laughed.

And then the door closed.

Chapter 12

STICK DOG PLANTS HIMSELF

Poo-Poo, Mutt, Karen, and Stripes all looked at each other in sheer and total amazement.

Stick Dog jumped from the front porch, skipping all three steps, and landed next to the gate. He looked through the metal bars to see if any other humans were coming—and was extremely thankful to find there were not. He nudged the gate, but it was definitely latched shut. They were trapped in that small space on the front porch.

"What just happened?" Karen asked, practically in shock.

"We got lucky," Stick Dog gasped. "Really lucky. I don't think that human could see or hear very well. I think she thought we were little humans in dog costumes."

"Humans in dog costumes? That's ridiculous!" Poo-Poo said. He seemed actually offended by such an idea. "Humans could never disguise themselves as dogs. They can't run as fast as us for one thing.

And the scent alone would give them away. We all have wonderful, distinctive aromas. And humans? Hmmph! They all smell like a soap factory. Yuck!"

Poo-Poo's disgust and commentary would have likely continued, but it was interrupted by a single sound.

CRUNCH!

Stripes took the first bite of her caramel-covered apple.

The others turned to look at her. They had never seen, smelled, or tasted such an apple before. They were curious and intrigued by it.

Stripes didn't say anything. She dropped the apple from her mouth and turned quickly to face the others. She closed her eyes as she chewed and swallowed—and smiled. In three seconds, she took her second bite.

That was all the information Poo-Poo, Karen, and Mutt needed. They began crunching and licking and munching. Even Stick Dog delayed formulating an escape plan to eat his caramel-covered apple.

In just a few minutes, the apples were all consumed.

"Oh, man. That was amazing," Poo-Poo sighed. He lifted his head and closed his eyes. He allowed the flavor to linger in his mouth. He wanted to savor it as long as he could. "That combination of tartness and sweetness is something I've never experienced before. The crispy apple and gooey coating created a swirling flavor sensation that awakened my taste buds and satisfied my belly. It was as if—"

But Poo-Poo did not continue his most excellent description.

There was a reason for that.

Stick Dog interrupted him.

"We have to get out of here!" he said urgently. "There will be more humans coming anytime! We have to get this gate open!"

The other dogs saw the concern and heard the anxiety in Stick Dog's voice. He didn't often panic. He was always the one who kept his cool. But right now, trapped in this enclosed space, even Stick Dog looked—and sounded—worried. This served to ratchet up the concern among the others instantly.

Poo-Poo left his food description talents behind and volunteered to open the gate himself. "Stick Dog?" he asked.

"Yes?"

"Do you want me to bash my head into the gate?" Poo-Poo asked. He lowered his head and stiffened his shoulders. It was the familiar head-smashing-into-something stance they had all seen before. "I could probably build up some sprinting speed from the porch and leap into the gate. That might help."

Stick Dog shook his head. "No, Poo-Poo. It's a metal gate. I don't think it would budge. And I think it would really, really hurt."

"Suit yourself. But I'm here if you need me," Poo-Poo said, and sat down on his hindquarters. He began to lick the Popsicle stick that had been stuck into his apple. He could still taste the remnants of the flavor. He sighed. "Mm-mmm. Apple and drippy goo."

Stripes, Mutt, and Karen saw that Poo-Poo had discovered some remaining flavor on his stick and began licking their own sticks with great vigor and satisfaction.

"You guys!" Stick Dog said. "Put the sticks away! We have to figure out how to get out of here. Fast!"

Mutt quickly took the stick from his mouth and tucked it into his fur for safekeeping.

"Can you hold mine too?" Karen asked Mutt. "I want to save it for a late-night snack."

Mutt nodded.

"Mine too?" asked Stripes.

"And mine?" Poo-Poo asked.

Even Stick Dog flung his stick toward Mutt.

"I don't know if I can fit all five sticks," Mutt said. He then looked backward over both his shoulders and then down between his front legs. He was obviously determining if he could carry the five sticks. To himself, as much as to his friends, he added, "I need to make some room."

Mutt shook his whole body in three short bursts of energetic motion. When he did, several things flew from his fur. All about him were scattered a broken coat hanger, a tennis ball with a long tear in it, a pen cap, and a half-eaten sock.

"There," he said, and smiled triumphantly. "Now I can save them all for you!"

Poo-Poo, Stripes, and Karen watched as Mutt tucked their sticks into his fur to be retrieved later for licking. Stick Dog, however, looked at something else. He examined the things that had sprayed and fallen from Mutt's fur.

He looked at all the objects and then he looked at the gate. He repeated this twice.

"The doorknob is metal and probably too slick to turn with our paws," Stick Dog whispered to himself. "And we can't reach it anyway."

Stick Dog tilted his head. He considered the dilemma for three seconds.

And then he began to move.

The others watched in silence. They were mesmerized—and confused—by Stick Dog's actions.

Stick Dog began pushing flowerpots toward the gate. They were heavy with dirt and withered, fading geraniums. He had to push the pots slowly in order for them to slide across the cement without tipping over. There were only four and Stick Dog knew he would need all of them right side up.

After two and a half minutes of pushing
and arranging, he finally had the pots in
the positions he desired. They stood in a
rectangle before the metal gate with each
flowerpot representing a corner.

"Stick Dog looks confused," Karen
whispered to Mutt, Poo-Poo, and Stripes.

Stick Dog carefully climbed up into the
flowerpots—placing a paw into each one.
They tilted and tottered as he stepped into
them. The old plants were dry and brittle
and scratched roughly against the pads on
his paws, but he paid little attention to
the pain. He focused solely on finding the
perfect, stable balance atop the pots.

"Stick Dog?" asked Karen. Her head was leaned over to one side. She tried  to figure out what she was looking at. "Do you feel all right? I think you might be mixed up in the brain or something. You know you're not a flower, right?"

Stick Dog closed his eyes for a few seconds before answering her.

"I'm fine," he said upon opening his eyes. "I know I'm not a flower."

Once situated securely, Stick Dog was tall enough to reach the gate's doorknob. He raised his front paws one at a time to the gate, pressing against the metal to maintain his equilibrium. He knew that if his weight shifted too far forward, or backward, or left or right, then his back paws would slip and the pots would kick out and tip over—and end this one opportunity he had to help his friends escape.

Carefully, very carefully, he slid his front paws to the gate's doorknob. It was made of metal and extremely slick. His paw pads gained no traction on the smooth metal surface. Even though he could now reach it, Stick Dog knew there was no way he could ever turn it. But he had expected just such a thing.

And he already had an idea.

Stick Dog called, "Could one of you guys bring me that torn tennis ball, please?"

But none of his friends responded to his request. They were too busy being confused.

"Uhh, guys?" Stick Dog called again. His leg muscles and back were growing tired and sore from maintaining that one position. But he knew he couldn't budge. He couldn't risk losing his balance. His voice sounded strained and weak. "The ball, please?"

"Umm, Stick Dog?" Poo-Poo said, and came a step closer. He was not bringing the ball. He stared at Stick Dog's paws. "You know those aren't shoes on your paws, don't you?

They're, umm, flowerpots, man."

"Yes, I know they're not shoes," he
answered quickly, and hung his head briefly.
Stick Dog knew he had to move this along.
Other humans could be coming at any
moment. "Bring
me the tennis
ball, would you?"

Now Stripes
came up close
to him. She did not have the ball either.
"Maybe you better lie down," she said to
him quietly. She didn't want the others to
hear. "I think you need to rest."

"Why?" Stick Dog said with as much
patience as he could muster. "Why do you

think I need to lie down?"

"You seem a little confused," Stripes continued. She spoke in a hushed way—like she was sharing a secret. "You've planted yourself in these pots, buddy. You're trying to grow more of you, Stick Dog. That's not possible. I'm surprised you don't know that."

Stick Dog didn't even answer. Instead, he turned to Mutt.

"Mutt, bring me that ball. Now. Please."

Mutt picked up the torn tennis ball and trotted it over to Stick Dog. It went from Mutt's mouth to Stick Dog's mouth.

"Here you go," Mutt said after the exchange took place. "But it seems like kind of a strange time to play fetch—what with us being trapped in here and all."

Stick Dog was extremely thankful that there was a tennis ball in his mouth. It prevented him from answering Mutt—or saying anything to anybody else.

He turned the tennis ball in his mouth until the torn side faced outward toward the gate. Then, gingerly, he leaned forward as far as he could and pressed the ball against the gate's doorknob. For a few seconds, it remained pressed in that exact position, but slowly—very slowly—the ball began to slide onto the doorknob through the tear in its side. Then it popped all the way on. Stick Dog opened his mouth and the ball

remained on the doorknob—and then
he leaned back again.

Poo-Poo, Mutt, Karen,
and Stripes all looked
back and forth at each
other. There was bewilderment and sadness
on their faces.

Poo-Poo leaned in toward his friends and
whispered, "He's really lost it, you guys,"
and nodded his head twice toward Stick
Dog. "He's trying to make friends with the
fence, I think. He gave it the ball."

"Poor Stick Dog," Karen sighed quietly.

Stripes and Mutt lowered their heads and
shook them.

"Stick Dog," Poo-Poo called in a louder voice. "That was real, real nice of you to give the tennis ball to that friendly fence. Real nice. Why don't you come down out of those pots now and let us figure out a way out of here?"

Stick Dog opened his mouth but not to speak. Instead, he bared his teeth and leaned forward again. He bit down on the fuzzy, yellow exterior of the ball. When he did, the rubbery inside of the ball gripped against the doorknob's smooth, metal surface. Maintaining his bite on the ball—and the handle—Stick Dog slowly twisted his head to the left.

When he did, the doorknob twisted too.

And clicked open.

Stick Dog pulled on the ball and the gate swung toward them. He let go and jumped from the pots.

Holding the gate open, Stick Dog turned to his friends. He said only two words.

"Let's go."

Chapter 13

TAKE ONE, PLEASE

After their escape, the dogs gathered in the dark behind a few mailboxes by the street. Overgrown bushes grew on both sides of the mailboxes and it served as a terrific hiding place.

"Did those caramel-covered apples fill you guys up?" Stick Dog asked.

"Pretty much," Poo-Poo answered. "But not all the way. I wish we could have just a little bit more of something."

Stripes, Karen, and Mutt nodded in agreement.

"Okay," Stick Dog said. "We'll be okay if we don't get anything else. But we'd like a little more. Another piece of candy or something, right?"

Again, they all nodded toward Stick Dog.

He poked his head out from between two of the mailboxes and scanned the street as best he could. It was still very dark, but the streetlights and porch lights provided enough illumination for him to spot what he wanted to see.

He pulled himself back and whispered to his friends.

"The witches are three houses down," Stick Dog said. "Let's follow them to one more house and see if they drop something. We've had good luck following them so far. If we don't get anything, we'll just head back to my pipe. Those caramel apples were enough to satisfy our appetites until tomorrow."

"Plus, we have the sticks in Mutt's fur," added Karen. "We can still lick those tonight."

"That's right. We do," said Stick Dog.
"Come on! Let's see if we can get
anything else!"

It took a couple of minutes for them to
stalk their way closer to the two witches.
They darted behind trees and parked cars.
They pulled themselves on their bellies
through the grass, careful to avoid the
house lights and streetlights.

When they caught up to the witches, they
found a perfect hiding place for observation.
A huge bunch of fallen leaves was piled
in the front yard of a small brick house.
When the witches were all the way up the
driveway, the
dogs dove into
the pile.

"Now, everybody, be very, very quiet and hold still. I'll try to see what's going on," said Stick Dog as he poked his head out of the leaves to watch the witches at the front door.

"Stick Dog?" Stripes whispered.

"What?"

"There's a leaf in my mouth. It tastes awful."

"Spit it out."

"Good idea."

Stick Dog could hear Stripes spit the leaf out. He watched as the witches approached the front porch.

"Stick Dog?" It was Stripes again.

"Yes?"

"There's another leaf in my mouth," she said. "It tastes even worse than the last one."

"Spit that one out too," he whispered in response. "But this time, don't open your mouth again after you spit it out. If your mouth is closed, no leaves can get in."

Again, Stick Dog heard Stripes spit the leaf out.

"But how will I breathe?"

Stick Dog closed his eyes and shook his head. "Use your nose."

"Good idea," Stripes answered. "Thanks, Stick Dog."

Stick Dog tried to see up to the front porch of the brick house. Leaves from the pile kept falling and rustling in front of his face, making it difficult to see. He tried to blow them quietly out of the way.

"Stick Dog?" called Poo-Poo from the middle of the huge pile.

"Shh!" he replied. "We're trying to be quiet, remember? What is it?"

Poo-Poo whispered back, "I think we lost Karen."

"Oh no!" Mutt and Stripes said in unison.

Stick Dog watched the witches on the front porch. They were not pressing the doorbell button or knocking on the door. Instead, they were bent over at the waist as if they were looking for something—or reaching for something. He couldn't tell what they were doing, but he was certain the door to the house never opened.

"Stick Dog, what about Karen?"

"Try to find her," Stick Dog said. "She has to be in there somewhere."

As soon as he made this suggestion, there was a wild and rambunctious rustling of the leaves behind him. It was as if the enormous leaf pile had suddenly come to life. Sprays of leaves shot out in every direction. A loud and continuous crackling broke the quiet of the night.

"You guys!" Stick Dog said as loud as he thought he could without being heard by the witches on the front porch. "What are you doing?!"

"We're looking for Karen," Poo-Poo answered quickly. He—and Mutt and Stripes—had not stopped searching. "Just like you said."

"Hold still! Please," demanded Stick Dog.

They did as he asked.

"Don't you want us to find Karen?" asked Mutt. He had remembered, at least, to speak in a whisper.

"Yeah, Stick Dog," added Stripes. "We're on a heroic mission to rescue Karen in this massive heap of bad-tasting leaves. And now you want us to stop?"

"Shh," Stick Dog answered. "Calm down, all of you. Of course, I want you to find Karen. Just don't go thrashing and smashing all over the place in this pile of dry, crunchy leaves. Every human out here is going to wonder what's going on. We'll get totally busted."

"Then how are we supposed to find her?" Poo-Poo asked.

"Call to her," Stick Dog suggested to his

friends. "Quietly."

"Why didn't you say so before?" shrugged
Poo-Poo. "That would have been a lot
smarter."

Stick Dog lifted his eyes and looked at the
moon. It was a peaceful and calming shade
of yellow. He inhaled and exhaled two times
and then answered, "You're right. It would
have been smarter."

Stripes yelled, "Karen!"

"Karen!" called Poo-Poo.

"Karen!"
screamed
Mutt.

"Shh! Stop yelling! Wait!" Stick Dog said as quickly as he could. "Hold still now for a minute. The witches are going to walk back past. Then we'll find Karen, I promise."

They all held perfectly still in the pile.

And the witches walked by.

"That was nice of them," one witch said as they passed by.

"It was," said the other witch. "Not everybody leaves stuff out like that."

Stick Dog did not know what this snippet of conversation meant—and he spent no time at all trying to decipher it. As soon as the witches were out of earshot, he called, "Karen? Karen?"

A quiet voice escaped from beneath the far side of the enormous leaf pile. "Yes, Stick Dog?"

"Are you okay?"

"Yes, I'm fine, thank you," Karen answered. "How are you?"

Stick Dog smiled. "I'm fine. It's nice of you to ask. You can come out of the pile now. We all can."

With that, all five dogs emerged from the

pile and situated themselves in the yard between the leaf pile and the front porch. With the moonlight and the porch light, they could see each other pretty well. And Stick Dog had scouted out their surroundings quickly. He felt confident that there were no other humans approaching. In fact, it looked to him like most of them were gone now. Perhaps, he thought, they were all going in for the night.

"Where were you?" Mutt asked Karen.

"We were worried about you," Stripes added.

"Why didn't you answer us?" Poo-Poo asked.

"Answer you?" asked Karen. "I never heard you calling me. Except for Stick Dog just now, I mean. I just heard a bunch of crazy rustling and stuff."

"Didn't you want to see what it was all about?" Poo-Poo asked. He was genuinely curious. "It was the start of our rescue mission to find you."

"Find me? I wasn't even lost."

"Yes, you were," Stripes, Mutt, and Poo-Poo said at once.

Karen looked at Stick Dog and then back at the others. "I was just being quiet and holding still like Stick Dog asked."

Stick Dog smiled again. He said, "Let's go up to the porch. I'm pretty sure there's nobody home."

They all followed him up the steps of the small brick house to the cement front porch. There, in the soft yellow glow of the porch light, was a huge plastic bucket full of brightly colored candy. There were lollipops, gummy bears, bubble gum, Sweet Tarts, and other candy. Sticking out of the bucket was a small handwritten sign taped to the top of a lollipop.

It read, "We're not home. Please take one!
Happy Halloween!"

Stick Dog reached in and grabbed a lollipop
with his mouth.

He then turned to the others. "Okay,
everybody. Take one," he said. "We're
heading back to my pipe for this dessert. I'll
lead the way."

It seemed like a shorter trip than usual. Maybe it was because the cool night air felt good when they breathed it into their lungs. Maybe it was the satisfaction of having those delicious caramel-covered apples in their stomachs. Maybe it was the anticipation of a delicious treat when they got back. Or maybe, just maybe, it was because they were all together—happy and safe.

Stick Dog climbed into his pipe first. Right behind him were Stripes, Karen, and Mutt.

Poo-Poo was not in sight.

Stick Dog leaned out of his pipe and cocked his head to listen. He could hear the padding of four paws coming closer and closer through the forest. It was Poo-Poo's footfall pattern. Stick Dog would know it anywhere.

He and Stripes, Mutt and Karen began to
tear the wrappings off their candy desserts.

"I wonder why Poo-Poo is so far behind?"
Karen asked as she bit through the wrapper
of a Sweet Tart candy.

"He probably found a tree to his liking,"
Stripes offered as a reason.

This made perfectly good sense to the others, and they continued to gnaw, bite, and lick at their desserts. It was another couple of minutes before Poo-Poo entered through the big circular opening of Stick Dog's pipe.

Clenched in his mouth was the humongous bucket of candy from the front porch of the last brick house.

"Poo-Poo!" Stick Dog exclaimed.

"What?" he asked, and put the bucket down on the floor of the pipe. He stretched his mouth open wide and shifted his jaw left and right. He was sore from clenching and carrying the heavy bucket all the way to the pipe.

"I said to only take one," Stick Dog said, and shook his head. He had just gotten the wrapper completely removed from his lollipop.

"I did take one," Poo-Poo answered after his mouth felt better. "I took one *bucket*. I'm going to share. Just like we always do."

Stick Dog didn't respond, but he did take the first lick of his yellow lollipop. It was the finest, sweetest thing he could ever remember tasting. It was lemon. He paused after that first lick and looked at the bucket sitting in front of Poo-Poo. It was completely, totally, absolutely full of candy. He could see plenty of lollipops—lots of them lemon—in that bucket.

"Well, that's true. That is what I said," Stick Dog replied, and smiled. "Good job, Poo-Poo. Everybody, chow down."

And everybody did.

THE END.